# Lynn Rowe Reed

# SHARK KISS, OCTOPUS HUG

## Illustrations by Kevin Cornell

BALZER + BRAY
*An Imprint of HarperCollins Publishers*

Balzer + Bray is an imprint of HarperCollins Publishers.
Shark Kiss, Octopus Hug
Text copyright © 2014 by Lynn Rowe Reed
Illustrations copyright © 2014 by Kevin Cornell
For information address HarperCollins Children's Books,
a division of HarperCollins Publishers, 10 East 53rd Street, New York, NY 10022.
www.harpercollinschildrens.com

Library of Congress Cataloging-in-Publication Data
Reed, Lynn Rowe.
Shark kiss, octopus hug / written by Lynn Rowe Reed ; illustrations by Kevin Cornell. – 1st ed.
     p.    cm.
Summary: Charlie the shark wants nothing more than a hug, and Olivia Octopus desperately wants a kiss, but
none of the people on the beach are interested.
ISBN 978-0-06-220320-5 (hardcover bdg. : alk. paper)
 [1. Hugging–Fiction.  2. Kissing–Fiction.  3. Sharks–Fiction.  4. Octopuses–Fiction.]  I. Cornell, Kevin, ill.  II. Title.
PZ7.R25273Sh 2014                                                                                           2012015323
[E]–dc23                                                                                                              CIP
                                                                                                                      AC

Typography by Dana Fritts
14 15 16 17 18   SCP   10 9 8 7 6 5 4 3 2 1
❖

To Jackson, Piper, and Amelia
—L.R.R.

For Kim, who holds my hand
—K.C.

Charlie the shark and Olivia Octopus were the best friends the ocean had ever seen.

While most other fish swam and played, Charlie and Olivia loved to watch the families on the beach. They seemed to be having so much fun!

More than anything, Charlie wanted a hug.

And Olivia desperately wanted a kiss.

They tried the obvious. . . .

But there were no takers.

So Charlie decided to put on a play. "Actors always get hugs at the end of a show," he said.

Olivia thought she would open an art gallery.
"Artists always get kisses from their fans!"

But no one came.

Next, Charlie and Olivia offered rides to the kids on the beach.

But none of the parents would
let their kids take a ride.

Still, more than anything, Charlie wanted a hug. And Olivia desperately wanted a kiss.

"I have an idea," said Olivia. "People love to eat. Let's have a contest to see who can eat the most! The winner will get a hug."

"And the second-place winner will get a kiss!" Charlie exclaimed.

Charlie and Olivia went to work.

Olivia was in charge of signs and decorations,
and Charlie prepared the food.

The next day, a large crowd gathered for the contest.
A little boy asked, "What is this stuff?"

Charlie could hardly contain his pride. "Why, it's the most delicious algae soufflé you'll ever taste!"

Everyone ran away.

Now Charlie needed a hug. And Olivia needed a kiss.

"It's my fault," said Charlie. "I'm the one who made the food."

"There, there," said Olivia, patting his fin. "It's not your fault if people don't appreciate good food."

But Charlie was heartbroken.

So Olivia . . .

. . . wrapped all of her arms around him.

And Charlie puckered up.